Jungle Doctor Paperbacks, No. F2

JUNGLE DOCTOR'S MONKEY TALES

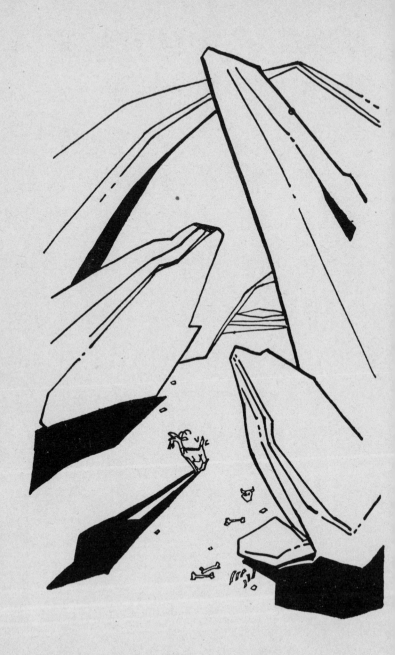

JUNGLE DOCTOR'S MONKEY TALES

Paul White

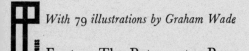

With 79 illustrations by Graham Wade

Exeter: The Paternoster Press

To Dr. Donald Grey Barnhouse
in gratitude for his book
"Teaching the Word of Truth"

ISBN 0 85364 145 5
Copyright © 1957 The Paternoster Press Ltd
First published May 1957
Seventh impression May 1970

This paperback edition September 1972
Second impression November 1974
Third impression October 1977

Australia:
Emu Book Agencies Ltd.,
63 Berry St., Granville, N.S.W. 2142

South Africa:
Oxford University Press,
P.O. Box 1141, Cape Town

Made and printed in Great Britain for
The Paternoster Press Ltd., Paternoster House,
3 Mount Radford Crescent, Exeter, Devon by
Butler & Tanner Ltd., Frome and London

Contents

Prologue

"DOGS are animals of great understanding," said Daudi.

M'gogo agreed. How often had he wished with strength for a dog of his own!

Daudi's voice broke into his thoughts.

"Behold, Chibwa has become the father of pups; this is the smallest."

M'gogo stroked the little animal. "*Hongo*, Great One, it is a creature of joy."

Jungle Doctor's assistant picked up the small puppy and put it into the African boy's hands.

Daudi smiled. "It is a gift; he is yours. Look after him with care, for he is new-born and of small strength."

"*Kah!*" gasped the delighted M'gogo. "*Assante Muwaha*, thank you, Great One. I will follow your words and will bring him with me to the camp fire at the time of telling stories."

The small dog licked his hand.

M'gogo beamed. "Truly he is an animal of joy."

Daudi nodded. "He will fill your days with work and open your eyes to many new things."

Chapter 1

The goat who wanted to become a lion

*I*N *the firelight Daudi looked intently at the faces of those who listened.*

He smiled as he saw M'gogo sitting on a pumpkin nursing his very small dog.

Daudi walked up and down, holding in his hand the miniature goat that Yohanna the chip-carver had made.

"Hongo," he said, "there was once a goat who was very strong indeed; such was the evidence of both eye and nose."

Laughter and a wrinkling of noses came from those sitting round the fire.

Daudi went on:

M'BUZI the goat tossed his horns and felt the comforting swing of his much-admired beard.

"Truly," he remarked to his shadow, "I am a goat of strength, a splendid creature indeed. Such as I should no longer be a mere goat."

He thought confused thoughts in his goat mind and at last from this whirl emerged an idea. In his loud and characteristic voice, he informed the jungle:

"I shall become a lion."

9

But nobody took any notice; they were used to the ways and the words of goat.

M'buzi was determined with the determination of his species. So he pranced along to the buyu tree where Nyani the monkey scratched with enterprise and result.

"Nyani," he called, "I wish above all things to become a lion. As a creature of education, tell me, how do goats become lions?"

Monkey hung by his tail, the better to muster his monkey wisdom. He pondered deeply and chattered in a knowledgeable fashion for a while, and then swung on to a suitable branch from which to explain.

"It is a simple matter, O goat, but there are many things you must do. Listen with wide-open ears."

M'buzi nodded his head and peered up into the branches—a position which he knew admirably displayed his beard.

Thoughtfully, monkey broke twigs and flipped them towards the upturned face. He held up his right monkey hand and spoke with great deliberation.

"For goats to become lions, behold, there are four rules. First, they must *GO* where lions go."

He paused dramatically and lifted the second monkey finger.

"They must *DO* what lions do."

Goat nodded and started to clear his throat, but Nyani went on hurriedly.

"Thirdly, goats to become lions must *SAY* what lions say."

Nyani took up a dramatic pose on the limb and waved his fourth finger.

"Finally, you must *EAT* what lions eat. Do all these things, and you will become a lion."

Goat's eyes rolled as he tried to contemplate.

"GO where lions go," he muttered.

"DO," the words were lost in a mumble.

"SAY," his voice became a trial roar that ended in the treble.

He stopped uncertainly, goat-memory failing, but monkey was ready:

"... and EAT what lions eat," 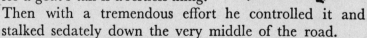 he prompted.

With a *mahhh!* of triumph, M'buzi set out, his goat legs moving in as lion-like a way as he could make them, his tail proving even harder to manage, for a goat's tail is a restless thing. Then with a tremendous effort he controlled it and stalked sedately down the very middle of the road.

In the shade of a boulder he stopped and spent no little time in roaring practice. His discouragement at the appearance of an occasional squeak was forgotten when he saw a large bone. Eagerly he picked this up and began to gnaw and roar, and roar and gnaw. After a most satisfactory session, he placed the bone carefully under his left leg and recited:

"GO, and DO, and SAY, and EAT."

As each foot sedately touched the road (he now moved down the exact middle) he said in a new, deep, goat-like tone:

"GO where lions go, DO what lions do, SAY what lions say and EAT what lions eat."

M'buzi stopped, sensing that he was being watched. With a small smile, he thought, "Ah, I meet a fellow lion!"

At that moment a long shadow stretched down the road. Goat adjusted his tail, gnawed his bone and moved forward again, his muscles rippling.

From his great height, Twiga the giraffe smiled.

"The sun has strength these days, M'buzi," he remarked.

Goat roared, and waved his bone in a menacing fashion.

"I am a lion.   I'm going to eat you, Twiga!"

"Yes, yes," came Twiga's sooth-

ing tones, "I understand. Now be *a* wise goat, go home, take two paw-paw leaves, place them on either side of your head and rest it on a cool stone. You'll feel better tomorrow."

Goat uttered a horrible sound that ended shrilly.

"I am a lion, a LION, a LION!"

Giraffe looked most sympathetic as he nodded his head kindly and moved away rather hastily.

With legs and tail behaving very much like any other goat, and with tears running down his beard, M'buzi rushed back to the buyu tree.

"Monkey," he bleated, "I have no joy, I am now the scorn of giraffe, and behold, I am still a goat, I've DONE, and SAID, and EATEN, and GONE, and . . ."

His voice was an unhappy, somewhat moist bleat.

Nyani considered the problem, scratching with care and without result, for the wells of monkey wisdom filled but slowly. At last the answer came.

"*Hongo*, no wonder, how stupid of me, of course it didn't work."

Goat pranced in impatience.

"What yet must I do?"

But monkey was out of ear-

shot, tearing bark from a tree. Then leaping to the ground for a piece of charcoal, he sat on a smooth rock working with great concentration.

Goat peered over his shoulder and saw strange marks which to him looked like the word "L-I-O-N."

"Wear this," said monkey, poking his finger through the bark and then pulling it over the shorter of M'buzi's horns. "There!" He stood back, admiring his work.

"You're labelled. Every educated creature in the jungle will know you are a lion."

A pleasant thrill crept through goat and he barely heard monkey say:

"And anything you might like to leave under this buyu tree would be appreciated."

Thinking lion thoughts, he moved through the jungle, his tail moving to and fro in the approved way, his pace exactly that of the king of beasts, his bleat growing more of a roar with every step, while the way he gnawed his bone was all that could be asked of any lion.

"GO, and DO, and EAT, and SAY," he muttered to himself.

M'buzi's eyes gleamed as he saw a movement in the shadow. Here was one of his new species. He moved forward, but mild disgust wrinkled his nose when he saw that the animal coming down the road towards him was Zebra.

The Striped One stopped and looked at him rather

anxiously.   Goat gnawed and roared in what he felt was the best lion tradition.

Zebra smiled. "The sun's very hot these days, O goat. Do you think it is wise for you to go out in the middle of the day?"

In as deep a voice as he could manage, goat said:

"I shall eat you if you're not very careful and very respectful.   Do you not see that I have become a lion?"

He shook his label under Zebra's nose.

"I GO where lions go, I DO what lions do, I EAT what lions eat and I SAY what lions say."

Zebra nodded.   "Of course you do, but now go home and wrap your head in paw-paw leaves and rest it on a nice cool stone and you'll feel . . ."

Goat's tail twitched most goatily and he rushed down the road in a rage, his label flying unread in the wind.   Zebra

looked after him and laughed till his stripes got tangled on his shaking skin.

On walked M'buzi towards the place where lions lived, roaring most convincingly. He strode round a great rock. It was a place of echoes and his roaring reverberated, especially in a shaded cavern.

Goat adjusted his label and carefully went through his routine.

"Is there a lion in the house?" His voice was unnaturally deep.

"Is there a lion in the house?" replied the echo.

M'buzi felt his hide creep and goose-pimples appeared in his more delicate sections.

"Is there a l . . . i . . . o . . . n," he roared, and his ears were charmed by the way the echo treated his voice.

But he was startled as the volume grew and grew when his lips had long been silent.

In the tawny sunlight, a large shadow moved, then came M'buzi's voice again, slightly high pitched.

"I have become a lion. . . ."

He stopped suddenly, seeing a great tail moving majestically. A singularly unbrotherly feeling gripped him as hot, hungry breath swept into his face, and huge paws hurtled at him, striking off his label. The cavern overflowed with thunderous noise which slowly settled into the well ordered sound of the movement of powerful jaws.

Goat had become——

DAUDI hesitated. M'gogo's eager voice broke in:
". . . had become a lion's dinner!"

"Truly," smiled the hospital assistant. "There is only one way that a goat could become a lion."

There was a pause.

A voice replied, "The only way would be for goat to be born a second time as a lion cub."

Daudi was on his feet.

"Right," he said, "that's just it. These are the very words of Jesus Himself, 'You must be born again,' if you are to become a Christian. Jesus was crucified and came back to life, not to produce better men of the old kind, but a new kind of men.

"It is mere monkey-wisdom to think that you can become a Christian by doing things, and saying things, even saying them with eyes that turn upwards."

Those that listened sat very still.

"There is small satisfaction in following the combined wisdom of goat and monkey."

Chapter 2

The monkey in the lion's skin

YOHANNA, the lame chip-carver, sat under the shade of the pomegranate tree and whittled and worked and whistled. Soon he was surrounded by those who sat cross-legged and watched.

"What does your knife make, O Fundi?" asked one.

A smile came over the quiet face. "This evening when the camp-fire is lighted, you will understand. I will tell you the story of Tutu and his need of a new nature."

All day long Yohanna sat in the shade, carving. At sunset he held a wooden elephant with anger written in every curve of

him, from the tip of his trunk to the end of his tail.   It seemed to quiver with rage in the flickering of the fire-light.

M'gogo whispered to his small dog.   "It looks fierce, but do not have fear, it is merely wood."

"Why, O Fundi, has elephant great anger?" asked one as Daudi came and sat beside Yohanna, who smiled at him, and started:

TUTU the monkey walked through the jungle with small joy.   The unhappy end of goat caused great sadness to weigh heavily upon his monkey mind.

"Goat was too careless," he muttered; "with a little more care all would have gone well."

He sighed deeply and climbed the buyu tree that grew near the house of M'shale the hunter, and sat nervously nibbling the end of his tail.

But monkey memory is little better than monkey wisdom, and soon he left off nibbling to chatter with rising interest as he watched the hunter's wife put a lion-skin in the sun to bring discomfort to the many dudus that hid within it.

The children of the village played beneath the buyu tree.   The hunter's smallest son put the lion-skin over his shoulder and tried to scare the others.

Tutu's eyes gleamed as the thought came to him, "Dressed in a lion-skin, I shall be a new creature and be even as lions are."   He leapt from the limb, snatched the

tawny skin from the astonished child and scampered off towards his family tree, his mind working very fast, monkey-fashion.

Twiga the giraffe, with his long-necked and inexperienced nephew 'Raff, stood amongst the thornbush, watching. They smiled as Tutu stood on a broad limb and fitted the skin round him.

"Not quite his size!" whispered 'Raff.

Twiga nodded. "But he really thinks he is a lion."

'Raff's ears twitched in a way that showed what he thought.

Four giraffe eyes suddenly turned to the place near the rubbish tip where Mbisi the hyaena snoozed, surrounded by flies. To his nose came the smell of lion, which brought loud warning to his twisted mind. There was also a strong aroma of monkey, but the whole jungle was riddled with monkeys. His mind turned only to lions as he hastily slunk off to the deep hole where he lived.

He did not look; his nose had warned him and he well knew that the legs of hyaena are shorter than those of lion.

Tutu was delighted as he watched the scavenger of the

jungle creep into his lair.   He wriggled with importance
inside the ill-fitting skin and chuckled with monkey mirth.

"Hyaena thought I was a lion; surely my new skin
makes all the difference."

Twiga bent his long neck several feet to whisper in
the ear of his nephew, "It is a matter of small difficulty
to take in those that merely follow their noses and do not
use their eyes."

Small giraffe stood on his unstable legs and nodded
his head as he watched Tutu climb the baobab tree to a
place where there was a large hole in the trunk.

Monkey sat with his head very close to the hole.   For
a time he moved his mouth very widely open and then
roared with no little skill.

"*Eh-heh!*" remarked Twiga, "a very fair imitation of
the voice of a lion."

The sound brought terror to the ears of Budi the bat and
his family, who spent the daytime in the hollow of this tree.

The thoughts in Tutu's mind were, "Budi will have
fear, and will certainly think I am a lion, for what but a
lion can be in a lion-skin?"

Budi certainly had fear, for he well remembered when,
as a batlet, he had heard the same noise and had seen a
great paw groping inside the cave where he lived, for
Simba the lion had an enquiring mind and wondered
greatly why the winged animals slept feet up and head
down.

In panic, the bats flew one by one through the hole in
the baobab tree, their darkness-loving eyes dazzled by the
glare of the sun.   They did not take in the fact that it is
a strange lion who swings by its tail from the limb

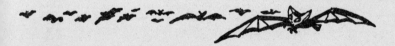

of a buyu tree, chuckling monkey-fashion.

Tutu was delighted. He told himself, "I'm very different and important and awe-inspiring in my new covering!"

Twiga licked his lips with his long black tongue and remarked, "A convincing voice, but to any but the dazzled, the sight would surely not carry conviction."

Thoroughly content with the result, Tutu thought little of the sweat that ran from his body, or of the irritable antics of Cockroach, who found novelty in climbing over the bumpy bits of his spine.

Tutu twined his tail more firmly round the worn ends of lion's skin and sought out Lwa-lwa, the tortoise, who quickly drew his head under his large shell.

Two bright eyes from this vantage point watched cautiously and twinkled when they saw monkey paws under the tawny skin. Tutu walked with the soundlessness of a hunting lion.

Tortoise smiled under the shade of his shell and watched the glee on Tutu's clammy face as he muttered,

"I have brought fear even to the cunning tortoise. Truly, if I'm in a lion-skin I must be a lion."

Again the giraffe's necks were close together and the words came, "O nephew, follow the wisdom of tortoise; silence is preferable when you see those who merely deceive themselves."

The jungle resounded to the trumpeting of Nhembo the elephant, who broke great limbs off trees as he lumbered along. He was feeling the heat, and was irked by a throbbing tusk. He flapped his great ears and his tail swished uneasily. Suddenly, he stopped, blinked his small eyes, and twitched his trunk in bewilderment, for on the buyu tree before him on a narrow limb squatted a shabby and tattered lion.

Elephant brought his trunk near to his left ear and murmured to himself, "I must tell my wife about this."

Then he stopped and muttered, "But if I say I saw a lion up a tree, then I shall be reminded in many words of the pink elephant, that disreputable member of my species seen only by the hairless ones after many days of celebration."

A deep blush of anger came under his grey skin. He looked just like the angry elephant Yohanna had spent the day carving. He filled his trunk with dust and trumpeted with noticeably small good-will. His words could be heard even beyond the dry river.

"Monkey of minute mind and infinitesimal mentality . . ."

Twiga murmured, "Hard words those, even for an experienced elephant."

Elephant went on loudly, ". . . your ability to deceive is of the sort unfairly ascribed to Ostrich."

With deliberation and care, he again filled his trunk with dust. With it he blew dust rings which framed Tutu in a way that offended his dignity, and to those who watched, made his monkey wisdom seem all the more ridiculous.

On a limb opposite him, Waa the hornbill, Suku the parrot and Mizi the rainbird laughed till tears ran down their beaks.

As the shadows grew longer, giraffe, in a gentle voice, said, "O Tutu, do you not remember the unhappy end of Goat, who tried to become a lion by doing things?"

Small monkey nodded. "But he was careless; I wear a lion-skin, and that makes all the difference."

Twiga sighed. "An insect-nibbled lion-skin, insecurely attached, has little merit. Even now the jungle laughs."

"But, O long-necked one, surely a new skin makes a new animal?"

Giraffe spoke very patiently. "You can wear the hide of Rhino, but inside you will still be monkey. You may

wear the feathers of Ostrich, but you
will not become a bird. You may crawl
right into the skin of Nzoka the snake,
and hiss horribly, but you will still
remain plain monkey."

Twiga was about to speak of spotted,
striped and mottled skins, but his
thoughts and words were interrupted
by the giggling of little monkey. "Did
you see hyaena run, Twiga? He
thought I was a lion, the skin deceived . . ."

Giraffe stamped his forefeet and
swished his tail with no small irritation.
"To wear a new skin is not to change
you. You need to be *all* new to be a
new creature."

But such is monkey wisdom that
already the mind of Tutu was thinking
how to make his lion-skin a better fit.

He spent the time of sunsetting and
the first hour after daybreak making careful alterations to
the tawny hide. He murmured again and again, "Goat
didn't do it properly, he was not thorough enough."

He rubbed some places with coconut oil to increase
their flexibility and then pinned the skin carefully in
place with long, sharp thorns.

Tutu wriggled till he was less uncomfortable, and told
himself, "With a skin fitting as well as this, everyone will
see that I am now a lion."

Completely satisfied, he walked beneath the buyu tree
making roaring noises.

Suku the parrot screeched in alarm. Tutu, with
lion-like calm, looked in the direction in which the bird's

great beak pointed. Then, in a twinkling, the jungle saw the unusual sight of an oddly-shaped lion scuttling up a tree, inches ahead of the unfriendly claws of Chewi the leopard.

"But who," as Twiga later remarked to 'Raff, "could expect leopard to understand monkey wisdom?"

*D*AUDI *threw sticks on the fire. The jungle noises came clearly, then he spoke.*

"You have heard of the false wisdom of both goat and monkey. This is a double reminder. Let your memory hold the matter with both its hands."

He stood up. "The wearing of skins is a futile attempt to become a new creature. The name of the skin may sound very good. Names like 'respectability' or 'the golden rule' ring well in the ear. The skin is good, but wearing it does not change the wearer.

"There are no two ways about it. Patched-up lives are no good to God. It's not repairs or reclothing or redecorating you need. The Bible says plainly:

"'If any man be in Christ, he is a new creature; old things are passed away, and behold all things are become new.'"

Chapter 3

Nyani and the matter of eggs

*D*AUDI *was walking over from the hospital in the evening dusk. Yohanna, who was sitting by the camp-fire, called to him and said :*

"Great One, and mixer of medicines, tell me, how may a good egg become bad?"

"Yoh," said Daudi, "that is a simple matter. Just leave it, and it will go bad by itself."

A chuckle went round the fire. Then Yohanna spoke again :

"How may a bad egg become good?"

There was a ripple of laughter. "This does not happen," said one.

Yohanna leaned forward on his lame leg. "Truly, in the matter of eggs it doesn't, but in the matter of men's lives it does. All are bad, for God's Book says, 'There is none righteous, no not one.' But a bad life can become a good life through the power of God.

"Sit down and listen to the matter of Nyani and the eggs."

*T*wo small monkeys, Pupu and Oho, crept down the limb of the buyu tree.

There before them strutted Crow.

Pupu placed his lips near his little sister's ear and

whispered the monkey proverb, 'where there is itch, there are dudus'.

She nodded.   It was common experience and a well-known saying.

Pupu went on.   "Also, O Oho, where you see birds you find eggs."

He looked with care and his eyes lit up as he pointed with his chin.   "Over there, see it?   A nest."

Pupu swung through the branches, looked into the nest and came back grinning, clutching a rather soiled-looking egg.

He tossed it to Oho who caught it with limited skill and threw it back with such small accuracy that although Pupu clutched with paws and tail he could not hold it.

The somewhat soiled egg fell with a sickly plop and broke on the limb beneath.

From the wreckage came a message that was not food for the nose.

The little monkeys scampered off with their nostrils firmly held, and their consciences quivered as they saw their Uncle Nyani walking delicately along his special limb of their family tree.

In his left hand was an egg, still warm from the nest of Kuku the hen. His mouth moved in anticipation. With the utmost care he made a small hole in the larger end of the egg, and applied his mouth to it with both appreciation and concentration. His cheeks hollowed and his eyes stood out as he sucked.

Pupu and Oho joined the other junior monkeys, watching with envy and awe.

Skilfully Nyani extracted the last vitamin from the egg, coiled his tail suitably and then stroked his stomach.

"Eggs," he said in a voice used by those addicted to

public speaking, "Eggs, *hongo*, how they comfort the stomach."

Memory rippled the skin of his cheeks and he licked his lips.

"But certain eggs . . ." Nyani wound his tail firmly round the limb and shook his finger at the small monkeys, whose eyes stood out in fear, but he went on:

"Certain eggs are an offence to the nose, a horror to the mouth and an insult to the inner monkey."

The heads of the small members of his species nodded in complete agreement.

"But how can you tell which eggs are which, O monkey of great experience?" they asked.

Nyani scratched thoughtfully and chose his words with care.   He held an imaginary egg between his thumb and first finger.

"There are those who hold the egg between their eye

and the sun.   These are called those who look, but the sharpest eye of the wisest monkey may lead him astray.

"There are also those who listen."   Nyani held the imaginary egg to his ear and shook it.

"But the best of monkey ears may be deceived."

He leaned forward and spoke very confidentially.

"There are also those who crack the shell to test the contents."

"*Ooooooh!*"   Many small, wrinkled monkey noses turned delicately upwards.

Nyani further unfolded the matter.   "The way of experience is to take a large gourd, fill it with water and into the water place the egg.   Those that sink to the bottom are eggs of worth, eggs that comfort and bring light to the eye, joy to the stomach, and nimbleness to the tail."

Nyani changed his position on the limb by a movement of his left paw.   A harsh note had come into his monkey voice.

"Eggs that neither float to the top, nor sink to the bottom, are merely fit for gifts to those for whom small respect is felt."

One little monkey nodded most understandingly.   He had once delivered such a gift.

Nyani's voice became shrill.

"But eggs that float to the top—that float to the top, I say—throw them far with skill in the same direction as the wind blows."

The full meaning of those words sank slowly into small monkeys' brains.

*D*AUDI, *around whose lips played a small smile, turned to those who listened—"Because you cannot see through its shell you need to test an egg in water. But God can see through you. He needs no gourd of water to know your heart.*

"Remember, and think, as your head meets the pillow, that God sees right inside you. What does he see when he looks into you?"

Chapter 4

The catch in camouflage

*M*BOGA'S *small dog crept under Daudi's stool, closed his eyes and squatted.*

Yohanna laughed. "Koh, he thinks he is hiding from you."

He put down a piece of wood, which he was carving into the shape of a leopard, and peered under the stool.

"Yoh, heh, he hides with small skill."

Daudi stood up and stirred the fire. There was no laughter in his voice when he said:

"Listen everybody, the most skilful cannot hide from God. Hear the matter of the chameleon, the wilful giraffe and the leopard."

L WIVI the chameleon sat on a small branch of the umbrella tree and practised changing colours by moving from one spot to another.

Twiga's most difficult nephew stood watching him turn brown, then green and then yellow.

Chameleon puffed out his chest and said in a squeaky voice, "Turn your head, small giraffe, and count one hundred. Behold, I can hide even from your sharp eyes."

He moved to a place where brown bark met green leaves

and yellow flowers. He became brown and green and yellow in a moment.

Giraffe counted, "97 ... 98 ... 99 ... 100 ... Coming, ready or not."

He twitched his ears, his nose, and opened his eyelids very wide, looking here and there, but at first saw no sign of Lwivi.

He looked again very closely, and there not a neck's length away from him was chameleon, skilfully camouflaged and almost invisible.

Headstrong giraffe was peeved with the small creature's skill. With a flick of his nose he shook the branch and Lwivi landed most uncomfortably, bruising not only his pride in the fall.

Chuckling nastily, Twiga's relation said in an unnecessarily loud voice:

"Chameleons can't hide from me, BUT I AM DIFFERENT. With my yellow skin and brown spots I am invisible beneath umbrella trees. The sunlight and the shadows are a wonderful hiding-place, for my spots are shadow and my skin is sunlight. Even Chewi would

not notice me there. Truly I am hidden from the keen eyes of leopard."

These words fell loudly on the ears of Simba the lion, who lay unseen in the tall grass not twenty yards away from him.

Crow, who also heard this boasting, flew off to report it to Chewi.

Young giraffe moved to a suitably sized umbrella tree. He pushed his head through the top and began to nibble the most succulent shoots. So safe did he feel and so comforted was he by the sound of his own voice murmuring, "I am hidden, even from the eyes of leopard," that he failed to notice the yellow and brown something that moved stealthily over the deep brown earth.

Simba saw the lithe movement of leopard moving swiftly, silently forward, his eyes fixed on a head that stuck out several feet from the top of the umbrella tree.

Chewi crept closer, and his mind kept telling him how well giraffe meat suited his stomach.

Twiga's relation kept nibbling, his mind dulled by a false feeling of security.

Suddenly Chewi sprang. There was a crashing in the umbrella tree and a long, uneasy silence.

Chewi lay basking in the sun on a great brown rock; his stomach was most comfortable, his mind at rest.

Crow had told him of chameleon's downfall. He mused:

"There was small wisdom in Lwivi saying 'I can hide from the eyes of giraffe'. He was almost as unwise as that giraffe who boasted that he was hidden from me."

A satisfying, gurgling sound came from leopard's interior. As he licked his fore-paws he looked with satisfaction at his own spots, stretching his rippling muscles and noting how similar his spots were to the mottling of the rocks.

Chewi growled deeply in his throat as his thoughts went to the houses of men and those who hunted in the jungle with spear and bow and arrow. Then he relaxed and said in his mind, "Behold, I am safe. My nose is the

sharpest in the whole jungle and my ears tell me more than any other animal. By my spots I am better hidden than any other creature."

He purred contentedly and thought again. "Behold, I am more of a danger to the two-legged ones than they are to me."

He rolled over on to his right side and M'shale the hunter, who for an hour had been hidden in the great

roots of a buyu tree, took his opportunity and shot an arrow into his heart.

Nyani watched the hunter skin the leopard, and wondered what was behind that day's happenings in the jungle.

He thought how chameleon could not hide from giraffe, giraffe could not hide from leopard and leopard could not hide from the hunter.

"Truly, many eyes see those who feel safely hidden," he murmured as he scratched in bewilderment. He watched M'shale walk home to the village with the leopard-skin over his shoulder.

M'SHALE himself had been listening to the story in the shadows. As he got up to walk away as the story finished he heard Daudi say:

"The words of Jesus Himself are, 'There is nothing covered that shall not be revealed and hid that shall not be known'."

"Koh," said M'shale, "how will God do these things? If I wish, I can hide my thoughts because my face is smooth and free from anger and fear; surely I can hide from God?"

Yohanna merely raised his eyebrows in a question.

Those that listened said no words.   None were necessary.

Chapter 5

Nyani crosses the equator

M'GOGO *was worried. He came up to Daudi as he was making cough-medicine.*

"Great One, a voice inside me says that I am not a saved one. My heart has great uncertainty. I feel no different! I feel just the same as I did before I asked Jesus to take away my sin and to forgive me."

"You feel no different," Daudi smiled. "Then you have not heard of Nyani's safari to the equator?"

"Not yet," said M'gogo as he settled down to listen.

NYANI had gone to visit his relations in a part of the dense jungle, where the trees grew tall and the leaves were very green, and large butterflies hovered over the swamp and the water-lilies.

Here Mbu the mosquito lurked with those of his species.

Nyani, surrounded by a crowd of hospitable monkeys, went to a very large buyu tree. Many paws pointed to a large board

41

EQUATOR

beside the road, on which was written the word
'EQUATOR'.

"O Nyani," said his second cousin once removed, "if
you sit here on the limbs of the buyu tree, you, being
educated, will know that you are in the Southern Hemisphere, but, walk along this limb, and leap to that great
kuyu tree and you will have crossed the Equator and will
be in the Northern Hemisphere."

Now Nyani found this a strain on his monkey mind,
so he scratched contemplatively and looked wise and tried
to read the notice backwards. Then he ran along the
limb and leapt from the buyu tree. He felt no bump as
he crossed the equator and he waited in the kuyu tree
with great excitement.

"*Yoh*," he said when the shadows had lengthened
somewhat, and the sun had travelled along its path no
small distance, "your words may be true, O my experienced relations, but I feel no different now that I am
in the Northern Hemisphere."

"Truly, you may not *feel* different, but it is a
fact obvious to all monkeys that *you are now in the
kuyu tree*, and this tree is in the Northern Hemisphere.
How you feel makes no difference; geography is geography."

Nyani nodded, but his monkey brain turned over and
over most uncomfortably.

"Surely," he thought, "one should *feel* different in the
Northern Hemisphere?"

Then he read the notice again and
again, backwards and forwards. Then
he felt the limb of the kuyu tree beneath him and said:

"Surely, it *is* so. *I am* in the Northern
Hemisphere, *and* yet I feel no different."

"*H*ONGO," said Daudi, "*when you cross the line from death into everlasting life, you may not feel different at the beginning, but keep on travelling further into life. Do not cross the line and just sit, looking back.*"

He paused, and seeing M'gogo nod, said:

"*But walk forward confidently with two feet. The name of one foot is 'Bible' and the name of the other foot is 'Prayer'. There is no* may be, *or* might be, *when the Bible says 'He that* hath *the Son* hath *Life'.*"

Chapter 6

Monkeys find solid safety

M'GOGO'S *small dog had been ill. Over the African boy's shoulders was a worn blanket. Snugly inside was the little animal, its tail busy.*

M'gogo spoke hesitatingly. "Great One, it isn't that I still have doubts after hearing the story of Nyani and the Equator, but I would like to hear more on this matter."

Yohanna nodded. He stopped carving a giraffe with its neck at full stretch and began:

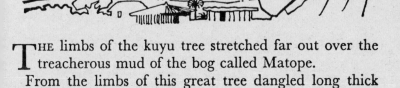

T HE limbs of the kuyu tree stretched far out over the treacherous mud of the bog called Matope.

From the limbs of this great tree dangled long thick rope-like vines.

Again and again Nyani had warned the monkeys of his family tree not to go near the bog, or to swing on the vines that hung so invitingly above the scum-covered surface. His words, however, had not taken root in the minds of Tali and Kali, the monkey twins.

Chattering, they climbed the kuyu tree with considerable nimbleness; down a limb they scampered,

nearly upsetting Lwivi the chameleon. They jumped on to the very end of a great trailing creeper and swung far out over the mud and then back, almost to the bank.

Lwivi walked jerkily down the limb and stopped where the vine twisted over a branch. Chameleon's unblinking eye noticed that with each swing some of the vine fibres parted, for Igwingwili the millipede had sharpened his teeth on that very spot.

Along the bank walked Boko the hippopotamus. He did not bathe in the mud of Matope, for he knew that it was a place of no bottom and that the strength of the

down-sucking mud was greater than his own, so he merely sat in the shade for a while, for the skin of hippos is easily sunburnt.

The little monkeys giggled and gurgled as their swinging stirred up the hot steamy air above the swamp, and they greeted hippo with words of cheerfulness.

Lwivi was interested to notice that the further they swung and the more often they did it, the more fibres of the creeper gave way.

Nhembo the elephant came lumbering down to a place where clear water bubbled out beneath a great rock. He drank slowly and with such odd sounds that the monkey twins did not hear the tearing of the vine above them.

Then Twiga came walking down the hill. They yelled their greetings to him and swung with greater strength.

Far out over the bog they went.

Chameleon backed away as he saw the last small strand of the vine stretch dangerously. The two little monkeys were swinging back towards the bank when a sharp sound came from above them.

The creeper had snapped.

They fell into the bog with a plop and immediately stuck. Their faces showed fear and then terror.

"Boko," they screamed, "help us!"

"How can I," boomed the great animal; "if I get into that mud, I too will be in danger of death."

They called to Nhembo. "Great One, help us with your long nose, we are being sucked down!"

Nhembo knelt on the bank, stretched his trunk

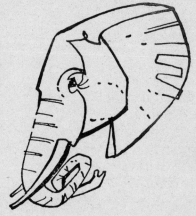

out as far as it would go, but their monkey arms at full stretch could not grasp it.

Tali and Kali whimpered with fear.

Then came Twiga the giraffe. The little monkeys were sinking fast, though they clung to the vine, which itself was slowly sinking.

"We can't get out," they screamed, "what shall we do, *yoh*, help us!"

Giraffe planted his front feet wide apart and bent down.

"Nhembo," he said, "stand behind me and grasp my tail firmly with your trunk lest I too should fall in."

Elephant grasped giraffe's tail and the long-necked animal stretched far out over the bog. His head just came within reach of the monkey twins.

Four monkey arms were instantly about his neck.

With the help of encouraging noises from elephant, and the screeched advice of Suku the parrot, the small monkeys were drawn out of the bog. Thick, evil-smelling mud stuck to them as they sat on the bank shivering with shock.

Giraffe slowly moved his neck up and down.

"*Yoh*," he said, "there is small joy in my neck because

of the clinging of monkeys and in my tail because of the pulling of elephant. Truly my spine has suffered insult."

Elephant made hissing noises in his trunk and rubbed his friend's long neck somewhat moistly.

The two small monkeys sat by the bank clutching each other, terror still in their eyes.

Mizi the rainbird and Waa the hornbill had arrived by this time and Lwa-lwa the tortoise had emerged from the shadow of a rock.

Still moving his neck round and round and up and down, giraffe said:

"Are you safe, small monkeys?"

They trembled and shook their heads. "We are not sure."

"Move over here into the sun," said Twiga, "into the very middle of this great flat rock."

They did so, and sat there still clinging to each other.

Twiga's voice came softly. "Put all your four feet on the ground firmly at once. Do they sink?"

The little monkeys shook their heads.

Giraffe went on. "Now, O Tali and Kali, with your feet firm on the rock, are you safe?"

"I hope so," said Kali.

For a while Twiga did exercises with his neck which comforted his muscles, and then went on:

"Put your feet and your tail hard down. Look at what they grip. Is that mud? Try to sink, try with strength!"

The little monkeys shuffled and scratched and then a slow smile came first over Kali's face and then over Tali's face.

"*Kumbe*," they said, "it's solid, we are safe!"

"True," said Twiga, "you are safe indeed. *The rock won't let you sink.*"

*Y*OHANNA *looked up from his carving and asked:*
"*Twiga was safe with his feet on the rock?*"
Heads nodded.
"*Nhembo was safe with his feet on the rock?*"
Heads nodded again.
"*And what of the small monkeys?*"
"*They too were safe, Great One.*"
"*Truly,*" *said Yohanna,* "*Daudi and I, we know our feet are safe upon the rock. The rock is what Jesus says He is like. You're safe with your feet firmly on Him.*
"*The words of the Bible are,* '*You are my rock and my fortress, you are my hope, O Lord, you are my strong refuge.*'"
M'gogo stood to his feet and said, "*Yoh, I understand, this is a thing of great comfort. Surely there is safety when your feet are on the rock.*"

Chapter 7

Famous monkey last words

D<small>AUDI</small> *put his hand on M'gogo's shoulder.*

"*If you want to have real joy in your dog, teach him to obey. This is also a way of bringing happiness to the little animal.*

"*Even Nyani realised this. Listen.*"

N<small>YANI</small> called together the small members of his family tree. He waved his finger at them and there was a look in his eye that produced mild shivering in the more tender monkey consciences. Nyani's voice was strong.

"A poetic elephant once remarked, 'It does not pay to disobey'.

"This is especially true of small monkeys. I have thought out three rules. Obey them and your skin will be safe, but do otherwise . . ."

He rolled his eyes and held up his first finger.

"Never stand near the hind feet of Zebra."

Up went the second finger.

"If your nose speaks the word 'Chewi'—leopard—climb with nimbleness to the thinnest limb that will hold you. Remember there is no laughter for monkeys inside the stomach of leopard."

Nyani swung by the tail so that he might underline his final point with all his four feet.

"And do not ever look into the eyes of snakes. Remember these words and you will save your monkey skin."

The little monkeys thanked him appropriately and scampered off.

"*Hongo*," said Twiga, who had strolled over to the buyu tree at the same moment as Suku perched on a suitably placed twig, "if I remember rightly, there were seven in your family, O Nyani?"

The elderly monkey nodded. "It's a sad story, O long neck. One stood behind a Zebra, three were careless in the matter of leopards and two looked into the eyes of snakes. I alone represent my generation."

There was sorrow in his monkey voice, and Twiga murmured. "You live through the triumph of experience over monkey wisdom."

"Pardon?" said Nyani, coming closer, his palm to his ear.

"I was only thinking in my throat," said Twiga hurriedly.

They sat and watched.

Two little monkeys were walking briskly in the direction of the place where Zebra graze.

Twiga rolled his eyes, Suku in anxiety bit his claws and Nyani groaned. They all looked up to where high in the air circled a vulture.

Nyani sighed again. "How well vulture understands the ways of my species!"

Two little monkeys talked together. "Why shouldn't we go near the back feet of Zebra?" one asked.

"*Koh*," said the second, "I'm not going to take notice of him; he thinks he knows everything. Come and find out about the hind feet of Zebra."

They came close and sniggered. They made remarks that weren't in good taste about black and white stripes. Zebra did nothing, except to reduce somewhat the distance between his hind legs and the giggling couple.

One small monkey picked up a thornbush twig, sidled

forward, and stuck the sharp point just above Zebra's hoof.

Twiga and Nyani and Suku saw a faint cloud of dust suddenly appear and a small monkey rose high in the air and then came down with a sickening flop. Nyani put his paws over his ears and yelled for Pilli, the medically-minded monkey, to come at once. They watched vulture sweep down from the sky.

The second little monkey scuttled for his life, climbed terrified into the family tree and cringed down beside his uncle, shivering.

Nyani merely said, "You saw. Say over and over to yourself, 'It does not pay to disobey'."

The opportunity to prove this again was given at dusk.

To Twiga's nostrils came the strong smell of leopard.

The noses of small monkeys told the same news. They raced to the slenderest and highest branches, clinging with tails and paws.

Leopard sprang nimbly up the tree and climbed higher and higher, his fangs bared, his lips dripping in anticipation of a meal of monkey meat.

"Hold tight," barked Nyani from a safe limb of the buyu tree, "you have performed with wisdom, no leopard can climb the slender branches to which you cling."

Chewi the leopard snarled horribly and used words aimed to produce both terror and perspiration in the small monkey, but Nyani's voice came comfortingly.

"Stay where you are and all is well. The words of leopard have neither claws nor teeth."

He swung a little lower on his limb, and commenced

making irritating gestures and throwing baobab fruit with remarkable accuracy at the enraged leopard.

"It pays to obey," he barked as at long last Chewi, snarling, slunk off into the jungle.

After a time of mutual monkey congratulations, Suku drew Twiga's attention to happenings of great moment in the place of great grey boulders.

"Nyani," he called, "quick action is necessary, or your tribe will decrease by one. I see a small monkey who looks into the eyes of python."

With a sound that was like the voice of Simba the lion, Nyani swung from his family tree and monkey-galloped to the place of danger. He leaped on to the top-most boulder and looked down.

Below on a ledge cowered a small grey monkey. The reptile slowly slithered its way towards its terrified, hypnotised victim.

Nyani tugged at a lump of granite with all his monkey might. It rocked and moved an inch. He heaved again. It skidded forward, rolled over, and crashed uncomfortably close to the great snake, who struck at it as it hurtled down.

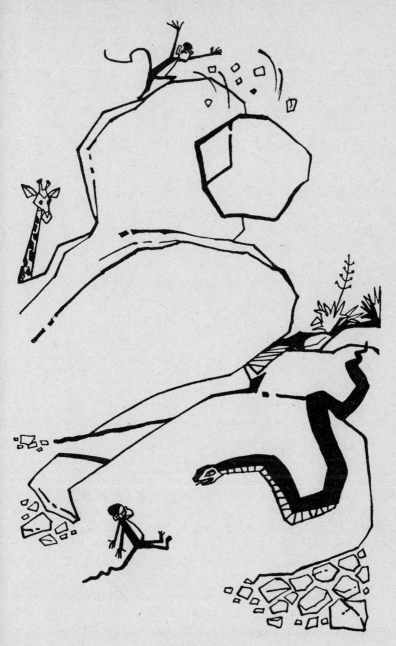

In that split second Nyani sprang, grasped the little monkey by the tail, and, barking triumphantly, leaped to a high limb of the nearest tree.

When monkey nerves had been soothed by a suitable diet of green caterpillars, in a gentle voice Nyani said:

"You understand now, O small members of my species, that it pays to obey."

The little monkeys nodded and looked with one accord at the spot where their small relation had sat yesterday— where he would have sat at that moment but for the flying hooves of zebra.

As they thought, they nodded again.

But Nyani knew with uncomfortable certainty that monkey memory is as short as leopard's temper.

"*EVEN monkeys,*" *said Daudi,* "*find value in obeying, and those who enter the Kingdom of God remember that this is the first thing that God asks.*

"*Does not the Bible say 'The man who claims to know God but does not obey His laws is not only a liar but he lives deceiving himself'? The more a man learns to obey God's Law the more truly and fully does he show his love for Him. Obedience is the test. . . .*"

M'gogo whistled to his small dog who stopped, turned, wagged his tail and ran to his master.

Daudi, Yohanna and M'gogo looked at each other and nodded.

Daudi picked up the small dog. "*Remember, M'gogo, Jesus said, 'If you love me, do what I tell you'!*"

Chapter 8

The monkey, the mirror and the red paint

*D*AUDI held a great mirror before him.

Those who came to the camp-fire crowded round to see themselves in it.

"Mirrors are things of wisdom," said Yohanna, who had just finished carving a small wooden dog.

M'gogo looked from the little large-eyed puppy at his feet to the wooden miniature in Yohanna's hand.

"There is another mirror which makes it possible for you to see inside your skin. The four-legged ones of the jungle will help you to understand it."

'VUMBE was a tan-coloured monkey who was interested in everything and who spent much of his time both in mischief and in rummaging in the rubbish-heap near the Jungle Hospital.

One morning he found an object that gave him no little joy. It was a nearly empty pot of red paint.

He sped through the thornbush, clutching his treasure and chuckling with glee.

Twiga the giraffe saw it all and thought thoughts of alarm. He bent his neck gently as 'Vumbe chattered importantly. Monkey wisdom and his strong curiosity urged him to wrench off the lid and investigate.

Giraff knew the worst had happened when he saw 'Vumbe's head disappear into the pot as far as his ears.

Slowly, an oddly decorated monkey face appeared. 'Vumbe could smell oil, but no matter how he rolled his eyes he could not see his face.

Twiga coughed a gentle cough and with difficulty kept laughter from entering his neck.

"*Kumbe*," he said huskily, "your face will cause your family no amusement. You yourself will have no joy in the hard work of your uncle's paw in the way you know so well."

The corners of 'Vumbe's mouth moved up and down and a tear ran uncomfortably down his nose. He dropped the pot.

In a small voice he said, "What shall I do then?"

Giraffe nibbled thorn-tree shoots and thought deep thoughts. He turned to 'Vumbe:

"O, ball of mischief, if you go carefully to the paw-paw tree at the hospital and look through the door you will see a small shining sort of window. Look into it and you will look back at yourself. This useful object is called 'mirror'. It is a thing of true wisdom. With it you will be able to see your trouble and remove it. That is the special and most valuable use of this shining thing."

Little monkey waited for no more.   He scuttled towards the hospital, going more cautiously as he came closer.

He peered through the fence, climbed it, looked this way and that.   There was the paw-paw tree, there was the door, and there was the window of wisdom.

He took a deep breath, bolted through the door. There was the mirror, but before he could look into it, voices came from outside.

'Vumbe grabbed the mirror and scuttled through the window, up the pomegranate tree and on to the roof.

"Stop, thief!" someone shouted, and a large stone whizzed through the air.

Over the wall, through a hedge, round trees he rushed, till he stopped, panting, under a jifu bush.

He was about to look at himself when jackal passed. 'Vumbe was pleased to see the way hyaena's partner looked at the mirror under his arm.   Even the wife of Simba the lion stopped and looked at him—a thing she had never done before.   Monkey then made a tour of the larger buyu trees to impress both friends and relations. He felt warm in his inner monkey as he saw eyes turn towards him and mouths that moved behind hands.

'Vumbe made self-satisfied noises which stopped suddenly when he saw Twiga looking at him rather queerly.

"Have you looked at yourself, small monkey?"

'Vumbe shook his head, and in so doing he noticed something dancing along in front of him.   As he moved mirror to and fro he noticed how it threw a handful of bright light.

Curiosity welled up in his mind.   He flicked the shining patch into the questioning eyes of Twiga who blinked and swung his neck sharply away.

'Vumbe somersaulted with monkey glee and dashed further into the jungle.

In the deep green coolness he saw Lwa-lwa the tortoise.

The flying blob of light flashed blindingly in his beady eyes. Tortoise's head disappeared quickly under his shell and his voice came shrilly:

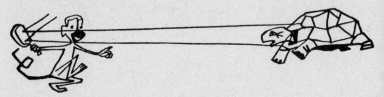

"Stop it at once, or I shall inform the senior members of your family tree."

'Vumbe swung by his tail and applauded his own sense of humour. He laughed till his ribs ached when he found that the light flashing in hippo's eyes made him sneeze in a way that reminded him of thunderstorms.

Twiga walked over to where mischievous monkey still swung by his tail and said very gently:

"Small one, you are so intent on mischief that you have forgotten the condition of your nose. A mirror is made to look in, not to play with. The light it reflects opens up the dark places. It helps you to see and avoid things of danger like pythons and leopards."

But 'Vumbe made a rude face and scuttled on to the top of an ant hill, where he saw Mbisi the hyaena winking at him.

'Vumbe came down to hyaena's level and heard his sinister whisper.

"O monkey, take no notice of giraffe. Do not look in that thing, or you will have fear."

'Vumbe shuddered and his mouth went dry.

"Wrap it in a banana leaf and hide it," advised Mbisi, slinking off towards the rubbish-heap.

Mischievous monkey decided to use it just once more when he saw his uncle Nyani comfortably and happily eating bananas.

The mirror moved in mischievous monkey's hand. Nyani blinked as the blinding light flickered into his face. He shaded his eyes and peered round to see what was producing the trouble.

Vaguely through the irritating glare he saw 'Vumbe with something dazzling in his hand.

Twiga saw that trouble was near and came closer.

Nyani continued to screw up his eyes and blink as the patch of light hovered round his face. Monkey words of horrid violence came through his clenched teeth, and threats that would turn monkey blood to water were directed towards gleeful little 'Vumbe.

With the skill of years, Nyani peeled an over-ripe banana, his hairy arms shot out and—*Wham!*—'Vumbe staggered back, tripped and fell, clutching the mirror over his head. His features were now decorated not only with red paint but with over-ripe banana.

Mbisi the hyaena laughed his evil laugh as he heard sounds of monkey misery mixed with the noise of hard paws striking with enthusiasm.

Twiga waited a suitable time and then came close to the tree where small monkey stood, for it was more comfortable that way, letting the cool wind from the jungle blow caressingly on his less comfortable portions.

Twiga said, "Small monkey, what is the use of a mirror unless you use it for its proper purposes? It is not a toy or an ornament or a charm."

But such are the ways of monkey wisdom that little mischievous monkey turned his back on giraffe, wrapped the mirror in a long strip of buyu bark and stuffed it in a convenient hollow in his family tree.

" *THE Bible is the Great Mirror,*" *said Daudi.* "*Read it and you see yourself exactly as God sees you. It is to be read, not merely carried. A closed Bible on a shelf does little for its owner.*

"*To make light of the Bible, to misquote it, to twist its words to suit your convenience are certain ways of producing trouble.*

"*Its own words are, 'The man who looks into the perfect mirror of God's Law, the law of liberty, and makes a habit of so doing, is not the man who sees and forgets. He puts the Law into practice and wins true happiness.*"

Chapter 9

The medically-minded monkey

"*Is it of first importance,*" *asked Yohanna, "to give a new shirt to a hungry man?*"

"*Or . . .*" *broke in Daudi, "do you first give him a pair of shoes?*"

"*Koh,*" *said M'gogo, "what do these words mean?*"

Daudi looked down at the small dog, whose left front leg was bandaged, and began :

G ROGI was a thin monkey of poor health. His unhappy state was in no small degree due to his stubborn refusal to eat vitamins.

One morning as he scratched unhappily, he heard Nyani telling of the enthusiasm of Pilli, the studious monkey, who for his birthday had been given a book called 'Medicines and First Aid for Monkeys and Others'.

Nyani told stories of great interest regarding Pilli's adventures and achievements. Grogi listened with ears that sagged and eyelids that drooped.

Suddenly he was aware of silence. He opened his eyes a little and saw a serious-faced monkey holding a book and looking intently at his sickly legs.

"Surely," thought Grogi, "this must be Pilli," as he watched him turn the pages till he came to a chapter called 'Sores, Scratches and Suchlike'.

Pilli carefully read part of it and then, brushing aside thin monkey's protests, he took a bandage from his black bag and bound up Grogi's leg in exactly the way described in the book. His work was considerably hampered by Grogi's inconsiderate habit of coughing and shivering.

This so irritated the medically-minded monkey that when Twiga gently asked, "Can nothing be done for his cough?" Pilli wrinkled his nose.

"Can shivering be splinted or a cough bandaged?"

He closed his black bag and stalked off through the jungle to find Nhembo the elephant, who fortunately was in an indulgent frame of mind. He listened to much talk and to many long words.

At last with a small smile twitching his trunk he agreed to be a model in the cause of science.

Twiga, Lwivi and Mizi watched with interest as Medically-Minded Monkey bandaged Nhembo's tail with great agility, carefully securing his efforts with a safety pin, and fortunately without other incident.

Inspired by his success, he proceeded, with a longer, wider bandage, to do greater things at the other end of elephant.

"Truly," twittered Mizi, "he works with skill."

"*Ngheeh*," agreed Twiga, "but the whole of health is not wrapped in bandages."

Next morning as Pilli worked on the legs of sick monkey, Twiga bent his head and murmured, "O monkey, do you not think medicines might be found to bring peace and comfort to the chest of your relation?"

Pilli stopped and looked long and coldly at giraffe without even blinking, and said, "And now perhaps you will be so good as to allow me to continue with my task in my own way!"

That night the sleep of those that lived in the jungle was disturbed by the bellowing of Boko the hippo and his numerous friends.

Amongst the umbrella trees Twiga shook his head, for he knew that bellowing of that sort always produced sore throats in the hippo family.

In the buyu tree, Pilli also heard the sounds and resolved to read the chapter on tonsils in his book, for

those who made noises of that sort always called for some form of first aid.

He had just re-read his favourite chapter when Boko arrived, his voice husky and his neck surrounded by a compress of water-lily roots.

Twiga saw him approach Medically-Minded Monkey, who listened for a time to his rumblings, and then said, "Open wide."

He held on tightly to hippo's large eye-teeth and peered into the depths as he told hippo to say, "Ahhhh!"

Nodding wisely, he removed the water-lily roots, and then he decorated the huge animal's neck most tidily with a triangular bandage, which soon was soiled in the swamp and did nothing to remove the unhappiness from Boko's throat.

At midday, Pilli came to bandage the legs of Grogi in the place where he sat propped up among the buyu roots.

Suku, who was most concerned by the strange wheezing noises that this monkey made, said, "O Pilli, is it not most necessary to soothe the inner discomforts of your relation? Are not some things more important than others?"

Pilli spoke no words, but the way he curled up his tail and the corners of his mouth left no doubt as to what he thought of the intelligence of parrots.

However, as day followed day, Twiga, from his vantage point above the thorn-bushes, felt growing alarm as he listened to the cough of sick monkey and observed how his ribs became more obvious each day.

"The matter of greatest importance," said Twiga, bending his neck down and speaking very primly to Pilli as he bandaged, "is surely his *life*, not his *leg*."

But Pilli tilted his nose in a superior way and said, "I will not allow outside interference when I am treating a patient."

Three mornings later he arrived with a paw full of bandages to find a group of serious-faced monkeys standing sorrowfully at the foot of the family tree. They broke the sad news.

"Grogi is no more."

Medically-Minded Monkey's nose twitched with anger.

"This cannot be so," he said; "I bandaged his legs daily with skill."

Twiga, hearing these words, murmured to Lwivi and Suku who were both on a top limb of the thorn-bush:

"Might it be that bandaging a leg is not the best treatment for what the tailless ones call pneumonia?

"You cannot tie death down, even with the cleanest bandages."

*T*HOSE that listened nodded their heads. Daudi stood up.

"Wash your hands by all means, but don't forget the dirt in your heart. Your body's health is much less important than your soul's. A man's house on earth has small value compared with his place in Heaven.

"As is the size of mouse to that of elephant, so is life on earth compared with Eternity. Concentrate on the things that really matter.

"The words of Jesus are these—'Seek first the Kingdom of God'."

Epilogue

M'GOGO smiled up at Daudi.

"*Hongo*, Great One, I wondered why it was you gave me that very small puppy whose eyes saw little and whose legs were too young not to wobble. But now I understand."

Daudi said nothing, but smiled. M'gogo also smiled and went on.

"With care and much trouble I have fed, washed and instructed that small dog."

"But when he was sick with dog's pneumonia?" asked Daudi.

"Did I not ask your advice and then gave him the medicine that cured him?"

The African boy rolled his eyes at the memory, for small dogs do not always appreciate medicine.

Daudi nodded. "You said you understood now?"

M'gogo nodded. "When my dog was new-born, behold, he was weak. Bones were beyond the strength of his teeth, so I fed him with milk and much patience. At first he could have been conquered by Panya, the rat, but soon he grew. However, even a growing pup has no chance with hyaenas unless his master is about or unless he learns to obey.

"As small dog grew, *kah!* there were dangers from hyaenas and leopards; there would have been great troubles unless my eyes had been wide open.

"*Hongo!* but how full of mischief he was! Sometimes his eyes were so innocent that I could smell trouble.

"Could the small dog deceive me in the matter of my

lost sandal or could he hide from me by pushing his front half under a grain-bin? Have I not watched him making up his mind whether to do right or wrong, to obey or not to obey?"

M'gogo drew little designs in the dust with his toe and said very softly, "My heart has had joy to see his love for me grow. I could measure it, because he wanted to be with me more and to do what I told him."

M'gogo looked up and smiled.

"You see, Great One, what I saw happen in my small dog is also happening to me. Was I not born a second time?"

He was silent for a while and then, "Your words and those of Yohanna make the eyes of my soul open and its legs grow.

"Does not God have the same problems with me as I have with my small dog?"

THE END

THE JUNGLE DOCTOR SERIES
Paul White

The Jungle Doctor books have become famous all over the world. Many changes have come to Africa since they first appeared, yet the instant appeal of a first-class tale, worth telling and reading for its own sake, makes them as fresh and lively now as they were when they were first published. A full list of titles appears below.

JUNGLE DOCTOR   0 85364 129 3
Christmas in Africa, with a thorn bush for a Christmas tree, and banana leaves as substitute for holly! Jungle Doctor, with a practice covering thousands of square miles, and an even larger number of patients, finds that the battle against tropical disease has its lighter side as well.

JUNGLE DOCTOR ON SAFARI   0 85364 053 x
"Sukuma" is Swahili for "push", and what better name could be found for the ancient car in which Jungle Doctor lurched from one crisis to another? Thrilling adventures could hardly be avoided in an unpredictable country where, in a few hours, a solid track might be changed into a sea of red mud, or a channel six feet deep might be cut across a road by flood water from the hills.

JUNGLE DOCTOR OPERATES   0 85364 132 3
"Do-it-yourself" could well have been the motto of the Jungle Hospital. A football bladder, some parts of a stethoscope, an ancient motor-car foot pump and an empty pickle-bottle provided, for virtually nothing, an anaesthetic machine!

JUNGLE DOCTOR ATTACKS WITCHCRAFT
0 85346 055 6
When little Mbuli was brought to the Jungle Hospital, everyone said it was a waste of time – the boy was bewitched, and would certainly die. But Jungle Doctor knew better, and soon Mbuli went home fit and well. Three days later he was found at death's door, abandoned by his friends. So the scene is set for an epic battle with the Witch-doctor.

JUNGLE DOCTOR'S ENEMIES   0 85364 135 8
A measles epidemic strikes, but Jungle Doctor finds himself fighting much more than a disease. Once again, Jungle Doctor and his African helpers find themselves up against it.

JUNGLE DOCTOR MEETS A LION   o 85364 136

Simba the lion-hunter nearly meets his match, but his life i
saved in the Jungle Hospital. But Simba has to learn that ther
are enemies more dangerous than lions, and better ways o
conquering them than the spear.

JUNGLE DOCTOR TO THE RESCUE   o 85364 137

When Simba the lion-hunter and his new wife Perisi go to liv
in an outlying village, their coming is deeply resented by som
who had made a profit out of ignorance and disease.

JUNGLE DOCTOR'S CASEBOOK   o 85364 059

"I will give you a cow for this thing", said the deaf man wh
had faintly heard a human voice for the first time in year
when Jungle Doctor yelled down his stethoscope into the dea
man's ear.

JUNGLE DOCTOR AND THE WHIRLWIND

o 85364 138

The lure of easy money overshadows the Jungle Hospital. Th
diamond mines and "the great peanut-growing" offer wealt
beyond anyone's wildest dreams. But wealth brings problem
with it, as Jungle Doctor and his African friends discover.

EYES ON JUNGLE DOCTOR   o 85364 139

Old Ng'wagu has his sight restored by Jungle Doctor and hi
"instruments of iron". But Berenge the witch-doctor, who ha
grown rich by his own brand of "strong medicine for eyes
sees his living disappearing as a result, and plots the old man'
downfall.

JUNGLE DOCTOR LOOKS FOR TROUBLE

o 85364 062

Trouble seemed to be in the very air, but it was impossible t
get to the bottom of it. In the village of a hostile chief a
attempt was made on the life of Simba, and Jungle Doctc
found him, with half an arrow in his back, only just in time t
save his life. The trouble strikes the family of the chief himsel
and Jungle Doctor is called in to seek it out and cure it.

JUNGLE DOCTOR GOES WEST   o 85364 140

Jungle Doctor is forced to take a rest, and goes off on safar
accompanied by young Mboga, who makes the breakfast toa
in front of a fire, keeping the slices already made warm b
holding them between his toes!

JUNGLE DOCTOR STINGS A SCORPION

0 85364 141 2

Nje – "The Scorpion" – has a special hate in his life, the Jungle Hospital and all who work there. The only person to escape his hatred is Staff Nurse Wendwa, whom he wants as one of his wives.

JUNGLE DOCTOR HUNTS BIG GAME 0 85364 065 3

Bill Bailey, an American photographer who is immediately dubbed "Bwana Kodaki", Colonel Johnson, a well-known former big-game hunter and Jungle Doctor set out on safari to photograph big game on the great plains of Tanzania.

JUNGLE DOCTOR ON THE HOP 0 85364 142 0

A feast of eighty-seven roasted rats enjoyed by the boys of the tribe is the first hint that all is not well, and when news comes of a village where many are dying from a mysterious sickness that produces many "swollen places", Jungle Doctor recognizes the symptoms of bubonic plague.

JUNGLE DOCTOR'S CROOKED DEALINGS

0 85364 067 x

Enter Goha, the tragically deformed but irrepressible little boy, and Seko, his dog. Both of them seem to be surrounded by crooked things, and Jungle Doctor straightens them out.

JUNGLE DOCTOR SPOTS A LEOPARD 0 85364 143 9

This story begins with mysteries – mysterious deaths, mysterious diseases, mysterious threats, and especially the mysterious tracks of a four-toed leopard that is threatening the village. The tracks come nearer, until at last the leopard strikes, and Baruti the hunter realises that he alone can tackle it.

JUNGLE DOCTOR PULLS A LEG 0 85364 069 6

The winds of change seem to blow as strongly through the Jungle Doctor country as elsewhere in Africa. New arrivals include the "little box" that speaks to Nairobi in a second, and saves many days journey, not to mention the con-man, who tries to sell four artificial legs that once belonged to his "poor dead brother"!

JUNGLE DOCTOR SEES RED 0 85364 083 1

This is the story of the Wadoyek, a tribe which stubbornly tries to stand against the tide of history. Proud, self-sufficient, these nomadic cattle-rearers in their red garments, their hair daubed with red mud, stride through the pages of this story.

JUNGLE DOCTOR'S FABLES
Paul White

These classic stories have a magic all of their own. Above all, they are characterised by the hallmark of all great storytelling – they are a delight to six year olds as well as to those ten times that tender age!

JUNGLE DOCTOR'S FABLES   o 85364 144 4
There was once a monkey who didn't believe in crocodiles – but that did not make any difference when he met one. Another monkey tried to pull himself out of a bog by his whiskers – all that was left of him was two small bubbles on the top of the mud!

JUNGLE DOCTOR'S MONKEY TALES   o 85364 145 5
Small monkeys never *could* remember *not* to get too near to the hind feet of zebra, nor to throw coconuts at Chewi the leopard, nor to look into the eyes of snakes. Fortunately, Uncle Nyani, the sole survivor of a family of seven, is always there to do his best to knock some sense into their heads!

JUNGLE DOCTOR'S TUG-OF-WAR   o 85364 146 3
Even by monkey standards, Toto was pretty dim. The Jungle underworld, in the form of Crunch the Crocodile, Mbisi the Hyaena, Slinki the Jackal, Vibi the Vulture, and Gnark the Crow think he will turn out to be easy meat.

JUNGLE DOCTOR'S HIPPO HAPPENINGS
                                      o 85364 147 1
Boohoo the Unhappy Hippo had a great deal of empty space between his strangely-shaped ears, and he suffered not only from hay-fever, but from an equally frightful desire to Help People, usually with unexpected results.

JUNGLE DOCTOR'S RHINO RUMBLINGS
                                      o 85364 166 8
Rhino has small eyes, a big body, a tiny brain, and a huge idea of his own importance. But his adventures turn him into a rather different animal.

All the books listed above are obtainable from your local Bookseller. In case of difficulty contact the Publishers at the address on the back cover.